LAYLA

CURVY GIRLS CAN - BOOK ONE

SADIE KING

LET'S BE BESTIES!

A few times a month I send out an email with new releases, special deals and sneak peeks of what I'm working on. If you want to get on the list I'd love to meet you!

When you join you'll get access to all my bonus content which includes a couple of free short and steamy romances plus bonus scenes for selected books.

Sign up here:
authorsadieking.com/bonus-scenes

LAYLA

CURVY GIRLS CAN BOOK ONE

A small town instalove quick read with all the feels.

Layla

There's a new shop opening next door, and I can't stop thinking about the bearded, inked owner with the rough hands. One look and my lady cookie melts.

But his noisy renovation work is scaring off my clientele.

Can I keep my customers, my heart, and my v-card? Or will I give it all up for one night with Kane?

Kane

I've got two weeks to renovate my new shop and get my business out of the red or it's going to fold. Not even the sassy café owner with the tempting curves and freshly baked goods is going to stop me.

But just one taste of her cookies and I'm craving more.

Can I save my business, save my heart, and get my hands on those curves, or will she shut me down?

1

LAYLA

The smell of freshly baked cookies wafts out of the oven and wraps my senses in a warm cookie-scented blanket.

I crouch in front of the open oven and breathe in the wonderful scent. No matter how long I own this cafe, I'll never get tired of the smell of freshly baked cookies.

The tray's halfway out of the oven when the hammering starts.

Thwack, thwack, thwack.

I jump in fright, and one cookie jumps off the tray and lands face down on the floor.

"Fudge biscuits!" I exclaim as Possum, the cafe cat, pounces on the cookie. "You're not meant to eat cookies."

The large ginger cat ignores me and keeps on

munching as if it's a pile of fresh fish and not a peanut butter and chocolate chip cookie.

"Strange cat." I slide the tray of cookies onto the cooling rack and crouch down to ruffle the top of his head.

Thwack, thwack, thwack.

Possum jumps at the sound of the hammer then goes back to his feast.

The hammering is coming from the empty shop next door. The bookcases rattle with every thump, and the wall shakes so much that bits of plaster dust are falling to the floor.

I glance around the cafe at my customers and am met by a sea of annoyed faces. As well they should be. If you've stopped for a coffee and some quiet time at Books & Cookies, the only reading cafe in Maple Springs, the last thing you want is a rhythmic banging on the wall.

"What's going on next door?" asks Janice, one of my regulars. "I thought that place was empty."

"So did I." If someone bought the place, then no one told me about it.

The banging stops, and there's a collective sigh around the room. Annoyed faces look back down at their books and reading devices, and there's a quiet shuffling as their owners sink lower into their bean bags or comfy chairs, which are scattered haphazardly around the cafe.

When I set up shop two years ago, my intention was

to provide an escape, a cafe where you didn't come to talk, you came to read. Armchairs, sofas, and bean bags dot the place, with low coffee tables providing a shared space to put your drinks. While quiet talking is tolerated, the cafe discourages conversation.

Most of my clientele are women, harassed mothers who can't find a quiet place at home, and older ladies who like company but don't want to talk.

I sell books, and promote local authors, but customers can bring their own book to read if they prefer. The principal business is the cafe.

Thwack, thwack, thwack.

There's a collective groan as the hammering starts up again.

"Do you think it'll be done before book club?" Janice clutches the top of her floral blouse with boney fingers lined with age. Her anxiousness reminds me that for some customers the book club meetings are the only social contact they get.

I will not let some thoughtless hammer-wielding person deprive my customers of social interaction.

"There's only one way to find out." I pull off my oven mitts and stride out of the shop.

I'm on a side street in town, tucked away down an alleyway with an antique shop on one side and a tattoo parlor across from me. It's the boutique end of town, the places you only visit if you know they're there. The shop next door has been vacant for months.

But today the cracked wooden shutters on the

windows are flung wide, and the door is propped open. Whoever's in here hasn't turned the lights on and I peer into the dark interior as my eyes adjust to the dim light.

"Hello?" There's no answer, and I take a tentative step inside. "Hello?"

The hammering ceases and a shape emerges from the gloom.

"Can I help you?" The deep male voice is deep and rumbling, like distant thunder, and it sends a delicious shiver running up my spine.

"I'm Layla. I own the cafe next door." I speak to the man-shape and he takes a step forward.

"I'm Kane." He emerges from the shadows with an arm extended. I stare at his outstretched hand, thick and worn from work with calluses on the palms.

Another tremor passes through my body because who doesn't love a giant rough looking man-hand?

I must be staring, because he waggles his hand reminding me I'm leaving him hanging.

"Oh," I say, gripping it quickly.

His hand has a rough texture matching its appearance, and I wonder what sensation it would create against my skin. Heat creeps up my neck, and I'm glad it's dark in here so he can't see my blush.

I drop his hand. "Are you renovating for the new owners?"

He chuckles and it's a deep rumbling sound, similar

to the sound Possum makes when he's purring on my lap. "I am the new owner."

I glance up at his face for the first time, and my stomach does a double flip because Kane is hot with a capital H.

He's wearing a jaunty smile that's half hidden by his rough beard. His blue eyes sparkle with laughter, and I'm not sure if he's laughing at me or with me.

"Oh," I say again, like a smitten schoolgirl. Then I remember why I'm here, and I force myself to appear stern rather than pathetic and pandering. "Do you have much more hammering to do? Because it's a reading cafe, and you're shaking the walls."

He raises his eyebrows at me. "A reading cafe." He seems to find it funny, which is irritating. But he looks so damn good when he laughs I forgive him, and then that makes me even more irritated.

"People come to my cafe for peace and quiet," I say, sounding pompous even to my own ears. "And I can't have hammering on the walls. My customers don't like it." I fold my arms across my chest and hope I look menacing.

Kane raises his eyebrows. "I have to get my shop ready for opening, so I'm afraid there will be hammering for the next few weeks."

"The next few weeks!" My jaw drops open. I can't have two weeks of this. My customers will head across town to Candy's Cafe. It's always busy at Candy's and not the quietest spot for reading, but there's no construction going on there.

"Can't you do it after hours?" I ask.

Kane's gaze travels down my body, unashamedly taking in my heaving bosom, pushed up by my angry arm fold, and my wide hips accentuated by the fitted black skirt that hugs my hips and flares out below the knee.

As his eyes travel over me the heat spreads from my neck all the way through my body until I shift uncomfortably in my bright red ankle boots. Damn, it got hot in here.

"I'll tell you what." He leans on his makeshift work bench. "I'll do my work after hours if you have dinner with me tonight."

I can't believe the arrogance of this man. "Absolutely not."

He chuckles and leans back causally. "No deal then."

My mouth drops open, and I can't speak. Kane's eyes crinkle with laughter, and once again I can't tell if he's laughing with me or at me. All I know is that I need to get out of here before I burn up with heat.

"I'm not selling myself to you," I say haughtily, even though my body is screaming that it would like otherwise.

I've seen men like Kane before, and they're not interested in me. Or they are, but only for one thing.

He thinks because I'm a big girl I'll give it up easily.

"Darling, you've outdone yourself."

She plants a lipstick kiss on my cheek, and camera phones are clicking again. Belinda turns to them because she knows how to work the media and starts telling them about the wonderful piece I made for her.

Phones are out recording this and it'll be all over social media within the hour, which is great for business. But all I can think about is the loss of Layla's warm hand in mine. And when I scan the room, she's gone.

LAYLA

I walk quickly out of the shop, managing to keep my dignity until I get out into the fresh air. Blinking back tears, I let myself into the cafe.

I sink to the floor as the tears flow.

When Kane kissed me it seemed so genuine, so real, and so freaking magical. For a moment, I almost believed that love could happen to me.

Then that glamorous skinny woman strutted in with legs to her ears and bare tanned shoulders whose bones you could actually see. The way she greeted him was familiar, and he embraced her back.

What was I thinking? Of course a man like Kane wouldn't be interested in a girl like me.

I've been so stupid. He only kissed me because the press were around and it would make a good story. When they asked if I was his girlfriend, he hesitated. Of course he did, because I'm not his girlfriend and I never will be.

Possum comes over to rub his head against my knee. I stroke him absentmindedly, but he keeps pushing his head into my leg and mewling at me.

"All right, all right. I'll get up."

I pull myself up off the floor, and Possum starts purring, glad his pep talk worked.

I wipe the tears from my eyes and pat his back. I feel a bit better, but it doesn't heal the crack in my heart.

I go into the kitchen and do the only thing that will make me feel better. I bake cookies.

I've got my hands in a bowl of cookie dough when I hear the door open. I must not have locked it in the state I was in.

Possum jumps down from where he's been watching me on the bench and goes to investigate.

I follow him out to the cafe, holding my hands in the air so as not to drop dough crumbs everywhere.

Kane is crouching on the floor, patting Possum who's purring loudly. Treacherous cat.

"I hoped I'd find you here," he says, straightening up. "You ran off before I could speak to you."

"I had to do the baking for tomorrow." My hands are covered in cookie dough, so I can't put them on my hips. Instead I lean my weight on one leg, tuck my elbows in, and stick my chin out, hoping he picks up on my "whatever" vibe.

"I'm sorry about earlier," he says, advancing toward me.

I shrug my shoulders. "It was only a kiss."

He falters, and his face falls. "Oh."

"No big deal." I try to sound nonchalant, because to me it was a big deal. It was a huge fudging deal. The first guy I've kissed since I was nineteen, and my friends dragged me to a dodgy bar and I drank too much tequila and threw up in the bathroom and then kissed a random guy. Yeah, after I threw up. Gross. So, yeah, this kiss was a big deal.

Kane takes a step toward me and the air goes out of my lungs at how close he is. "I'm not sorry about the kiss."

"Oh?" I raise my eyebrows.

Kane's eyes dart to my lips. "The kiss was perfect."

"Oh," seems to be all I can say. My insides are going gooey, and my "whatever" stance is crumbling.

"I'm sorry I was hijacked by Belinda. She's one of my best customers, and she likes to make a scene."

"She's very glamorous," I say hesitantly.

He smiles a cheeky grin. "Are you jealous?"

"No," I say quickly.

He chuckles. "I wish you were. It would mean you have the same feelings about me as I do about you."

My heart stops in my throat. "And what feelings are those?" I whisper.

Well, not me. Not me at all. I may be the only twenty-five-year-old virgin in the state.

Mom's always warning me I'll die alone with nothing but cats and books for company, which doesn't sound like a bad life. But there is a part of me that longs to meet someone special. The problem is that I never seem to find that person who makes my heart race and my knees turn to jelly.

Which is why I'm so disconcerted when I stumble out of Kane's shop, my stomach all aflutter and my lady cookie going all gooey.

2

KANE

*L*ayla sticks her chin in the air and spins on her heel. I watch her ass swing as she marches haughtily out of the shop, her figure framed in the sunlight.

My dick twitches in my pants; damn, she's a good-looking woman. Those full breasts pressed up against her blouse and her substantial ass that makes a man want to grab it with both hands. It's a pity she thinks she's too good for me and won't have dinner with me. Or maybe she's got a boyfriend, but I didn't see a ring, so that makes her fair game.

A smile plays on my lips. Layla may think she's too good for the likes of me, but I'll show her what she's missing. The game is on.

There are a few papers on the end of the work-bench and my gaze rests on the plan for the shop. I've still got a lot to do before opening in two weeks. I pick it up, and a bill falls out from underneath and drops on the floor.

I try not to look at it as I tuck it into my pocket. I don't need to. I know the numbers of my debt by heart.

There was a fire in my last shop, and the insurance hasn't paid out like it should. I lost some valuable pieces, and there was a lot of smoke damage. I need to get back up and running as quickly as I can, or I might fold for good.

While I want to be mindful of Layla's customers, my own livelihood is at stake.

I scan the list of jobs that need doing to get this place ready for opening. To save on building costs I'm doing the place up myself.

When I get to painting and decorating it'll be nice and quiet. But first there's a wall to knock down, a work bench to cut, and a lot of sanding. She's just going to have to put up with the noise for a bit.

I grab my mallet. Today I'm taking down a wall. "Sorry Layla," I say as I smash into the plaster.

It's the next day, and I'm in the shop early. I pulled the entire wall down yesterday and clear the debris. Today I'm sanding it back and cleaning up the edges.

I've opened the interior of the shop right up, so my workspace sits alongside the merchandise. It means I can keep working while running the store.

People love to come in and browse, and it means I

won't have to stop work every time there's a customer. Of course, one day I'll have a shop assistant and I can focus on my craft, but for now, to cut costs I'm doing it all myself.

I stifle a yawn and take a swig from my mug. My lips curl at the bitter taste of instant coffee. The first luxury I'm buying is an espresso machine.

I spend a few hours stripping back the wall and tidying the plaster around the new opening. It's 10 a.m. before I dust off my hands and pick up the gift for Layla.

The aroma of freshly baked cookies hits me as soon as I open the door to Books & Cookies. My stomach grumbles, and an older woman looks up crossly from her book. It's quiet in here, like a library, which I guess is the point.

The chairs are arranged haphazardly, which I suppose some people find cozy, but I'm itching to straighten them up. To put them in orderly rows. The coffee tables are shabby, and the chairs look like they were collected from the side of the road.

But every worn-looking chair in the place contains a customer with their nose in a book. The dim screens of reading devices are just as prominent as the paper variety.

The tables are littered with mugs of steaming drinks. My neck twitches at the sight of the mismatched coffee mugs. I like things in order, to be uniform. The disorder of this place is making me tense.

On one wall is a large cork board with community notices pinned to it. One bright flyer catches my eye.

Maple Springs Businesswomen's Network.

Meet the first Thursday of the month at Books & Cookies.

All Welcome.

It's not all welcome if it's a women's only network and I'm about to snatch the flyer so I can ask Layla if I can join just to mess with her. But when I turn around a large ginger cat eyes me from its perch on the top of an armchair. Its eyes narrow and its tail swishes as if daring me to break the peace.

I'm not about to fuck off the cat as well as the cafe owner. I leave the flyer and turn to the counter.

Layla stands there, hands on hips, with a questioning expression. She's wearing a tight fitting t-shirt with a pale pink floral design that stretches over her mouth-watering breasts. It takes me a moment of staring to realize the flower design is writing and another good few moments to decipher what it says.

I read smut

My mouth goes dry and my eyes widen. The thought of Layla reading dirty books causes a stirring in my pants, and I step forward before she can see the effect she's having on me.

"I came to give you this." My voice booms around the room, and the lady who gave my stomach a dirty look for grumbling too loudly looks up again.

"We encourage customers to keep talking to a minimum," says Layla, a smile playing on her lips.

With my size, rough beard, and tattooed arms, I'm out of place, and she's enjoying my discomfort.

I clear my throat and drop my voice to a whisper. "A peace offering," I say, holding a package wrapped in brown paper.

She takes it skeptically. "What's this?"

"Something made in my shop, for your shop."

She unwraps the parcel and pulls out the wooden bookends. They're hand carved with a swirl design, and the wood is polished to a sleek shine.

She turns them over in her hands. "They're beautiful. Thank you." She holds them up and examines the initials carved into the bottom. "KB. Is that you?"

I nod.

"So that's what you do next door? Make bookends?"

"Something like that." I make a lot more than that but I don't want to annoy her customers anymore but launching into an explanation of what I do.

"What do I owe you?"

Layla reaches under the counter and I shake my head. "Nothing. It's a gift."

Her eyes narrow. "Are you going to be noisy again today?"

I shake my head. "I've got the wall knocked down now. There may be a bit of sanding but nothing to make the wall shake."

"Good."

"I will have more to do later in the week though. I thought I should warn you." I open my hands apologetically. "Do you have any quieter times? Perhaps we can try and work around each other."

She looks around the cafe and sighs. "Just avoid the book clubs."

"What time is book club?"

"Mornings at ten-thirty and every afternoon at four."

"I'll try to avoid those times then."

"I'd appreciate that, thank you. And the Businesswomen's Network meeting."

I glance at the poster and note the time. "Got it."

The lady with the sensitive ears pipes up. "You two gonna gas bag all day? Because some of us are trying to read here."

"Sorry, Janice," says Layla. "We're finished talking." She gives me a smile and leans forward. "You want a coffee?" she whispers. "On the house."

I nod while trying not to stare at her cleavage. "And one of those cookies."

I leave with a good coffee, a chocolate cookie, and a painful hard-on. The cat follows me to the door, eyeing me warily as it escorts me off the premises.

3

LAYLA

The plate wobbles, threatening to tip cookies on the carpet, as I weave between the armchairs that surround two tables that have been pushed together. In each armchair sits a member of the Maple Springs Businesswomen's Network. A few laptops are open on the table and the sound of chatter and laughter mixes with the hum from the coffee machine.

I place the plate of cookies in the center of the tables and stand back, nibbling on a fingernail as my toughest critics select a cookie.

What started as an informal meet up with a few friends who were also starting up their own businesses has turned into a group of over ten local women who come together in person every month and more often online to share ideas, blow off steam, and test out my latest cookie recipes.

Frankie grabs the first cookie and moans as she bites into it. She closes her eyes as she chews, holding a finger up to indicate she's thinking.

She swallows her mouthful and cracks an eyelid open to peer at me. "Pecan and chocolate?"

Lizzie shakes her head and swallows her own mouthful of cookie. "It's walnut and white chocolate, with cinnamon. Am I right?"

I glance around at the group to see if there's any other guesses.

Maria's face looks pained as it stares out of the laptop screen where she's video called in to join us. "You guys are killing me."

Lizzie pulls a face at the screen and stuffs the rest of her cookie in her mouth. "Sorry, not sorry." She says between mouthfuls. "These are fucking delicious, Layla." She turns her sparkling green eyes to me. "I don't even want to know what's in them. Just keep them coming."

I grin at the women who have become close friends, enjoying their enjoyment of my baking.

"I'm definitely getting white chocolate." Ellie nibbles on the end of her cookie, then lays it down on a napkin, mostly untouched.

She's started training for a charity run, so I don't push it. If she can resist a freshly baked cookie, then she's got more will power than me.

"White chocolate in a cookie is my favorite." Maria says mournfully.

I make a mental note to send some to her office. Since Maria moved to Seattle I don't get to see her much, but she never misses one of our meetings.

"Dang it," says Ellie, picking up her cookie and talking a large bite. "I need the energy to run..." her sentence turns into a moan as the flavor hits her tastebuds.

I can't keep the grin off my face as the group devours the cookies trying to guess what's in them.

"White chocolate." I say finally. "Walnuts and a hint of cinnamon."

"Called it!" Says Lizzie, thumping the table triumphantly.

Lizzie always gets the flavors right. She runs a bath bomb business and has a good nose for separating different scents and flavors.

"Are they worth putting on the menu?" but I already know what they're going to say.

There's a chorus of 'yes' around the table. They always say yes. I've never served up a bad cookie, apart from the pumpkin seed and toffee I tried last Halloween.

I take a seat in a spare armchair and grab myself a cookie.

"Any update on the development?" I ask Frankie.

She's restoring her mom's beauty salon at the other end of town, but some snooty developer wants to get rid of the shops and turn the block into apartment buildings. The salon has sentimental value for Frankie and she's struggling with the idea she might lose it.

Frankie's brow furrows. "I've written a strongly worded letter to the developer."

"Did you say a letter?" Pipes up Maria. "Where are we, the nineties?"

The girls giggle and Frankie bristles. "An email is too easily dismissed. I didn't want Mr. William Fletcher to ignore me."

She emphasis his name and sits up straight in her chair as she sweeps her hair over her shoulders. I don't see how anyone could ignore the bold Frankie. But when you're from a small town taking on a property developer, you have to be bold.

We talk a little more about the decrease in footfall and Lou, another of our members, commiserates with Frankie. She too, inherited a business.

Buffalo Bill's is a Maple Springs institution, or at least it used to be twenty years ago when her dad ran it. Lou's struggling to keep it running and the entire place needs renovating.

The women offer advice and support and we all pledge to be available in whatever capacity Lou or Frankie needs us.

Ellie, now with only half a cookie on her napkin, tells us how her training's going. She only got back into town a few months ago and while she decides what her next move is, she's taken up jogging. It might have something to do with a certain ex-military neighbor of hers who's taking the running club.

"Anyone want to come jogging with me tomorrow morning?" She looks around the table hopefully.

"I'd rather stick my leg in a vice," says Lizzie. "No offense, sweetie, I'll come and cheer you on, but this body..." she indicates her substantial form squeezed into the armchair. "...does not run."

While the girls chat, I snag the last cookie and tuck it into a napkin for Kane tomorrow. I can imagine his face when he bites into it. He'll probably close his eyes and groan in that sexy low rumble he has that makes my core squeeze tight.

"How's things going with the guy next door?" asks Frankie.

"Huh?" I'm pulled out of my thoughts by her question. Is it that obvious I'm attracted to Kane? My neck flushes. "Nothing's happening between us."

Frankie's eyebrows shoot into her forehead and there's silence around the table until Lizzie erupts in a cackle.

Frankie slaps her hands together. "I was only meaning has he finished his repairs but if there's something else going on you need to spill the tea."

Heat creeps up my neck as I realize what I've said. "There's no tea to spill." I say hastily. "Kane is a pain in the ass who enjoys making my life difficult."

"Is that the only thing he's enjoying?" Lizzie waggles

her eyebrows at me and there are giggles around the table.

I can't hide anything from these women. We meet to support each other in business, but it's become more than that. They've become good friends. Still, there's nothing to tell. Kane is just a pain in the ass and the fact I'm attracted to him makes it even more infuriating.

"I'll get the next batch of cookies."

I stand up quickly and retrieve the empty plate from the table. The girls laugh at me as I head to the kitchen.

If there was something to tell, I'd tell them. But so far, all Kane has done is disrupt my peace, befriend my cat and flirt with Janice. Hardly anything to tell the girls about.

4

LAYLA

*I*t's almost a week since Kane exploded into my life, disturbing my quiet cafe with his hammering and sawing. Not to mention the way he's disrupted my own equilibrium with his tousled beard and rough hands.

No matter how early I get to the shop, he's there before me with the door propped open and clouds of sawdust swirling. He works hard, I'll give him that.

I open the cafe and get the first batch of cookies ready, white chocolate and cranberry. I like to vary it and give the customers something different each day. I make a carrot cake too, with soft buttery icing on top.

It's almost 10 a.m. when the door opens and his burly figure saunters in. My stomach does a fluttery dance, which is highly annoying, but something I can't seem to control.

The traitorous cat jumps off an armchair to greet him with a loud purr, and even Janice smiles up at him.

In the week he's been here, he's charmed even my toughest of customers.

He stoops to pat Possum and salutes Janice, which makes her grin so hard her dentures nearly fall out. If you've never seen a seventy-something lady flirt silently with a burly, tattooed, bearded man, I can tell you it's quite a sight.

He doesn't have to speak to tell me what he wants, and I start making his coffee while he scans the baked goods. He points at a particularly plump cookie, and I put it in a brown bag for him.

He hands over a ten-dollar bill, and when our hands brush, I get the same spark I do every morning. It shoots up my arm and sends a delicious shiver all the way down my spine. I wonder if he senses it too, as I hand over his change, dropping the coins into his thick hands that have flecks of dirt and paint on them. Workman's hands. I wonder what he'd think if he knew I've been thinking about those hands at night running over my body.

I sigh inwardly. He's flirting with me the same way he flirts with Janice and probably with all the other women who admire him but will never have him, the old ladies and the big girls like me.

He gives me a broad smile as he leaves, and I watch him go out the door. Possum follows him out mewling mournfully, showing less restraint than I do.

It's become our morning ritual and what I look forward to most in the day. Sometimes I see him when I lock up too, and we chat for a bit. But he's never asked me out to dinner again.

It's later that afternoon, and today's book club, the Romance Readers, has just started. It's a small group hosted by Janice. I've moved the chairs into a circle for her at the front of the cafe. It's the only time conversation is encouraged in the cafe, but everyone still talks in hushed voices.

Suddenly an ear-piercing noise shatters the quiet. I put my hands over my ears, as do most of the customers, but the screeching of the saw from outside penetrates my eardrums.

It stops for a moment, and I lower my hands.

"What in god's name is that hideous sound?" asks Janice.

"I've got a pretty good idea," I say, moving to the window. I stop dead in my tracks. Kane has a workbench set up outside with a plank of wood across it and a circular saw. And he's working with his shirt off.

Sweat glistens off his chest, which is covered in inked designs, and his arms bulge with muscles I don't even know the names of.

"Oh my," says Janice, which is an understatement.

Suddenly every woman and half the men in the cafe are looking out the window. Kane, oblivious to his audience, starts up the saw again, and my customers duck their heads, covering their ears against the piercing screech.

"I'll be right back, ladies," I say, although no one can hear me over the din.

I stride out of the shop and over to Kane. Just because he looks hot with his shirt off doesn't mean he can make a racket in the street.

I stop in front of the table, my arms folded. He mustn't have heard me approach, so I stand there like an idiot until he turns the saw off.

He looks up at me and smiles, which is disarming, because he looks so damn hot when he smiles and it makes my lower belly twist in the most delicious way. I ignore my damned gut and keep my arms folded, determined not to let him charm me out of my anger.

"You promised you would keep quiet during book club."

He scratches his beard thoughtfully. "I said I'd try. But I need to get this cut today."

"Can't you do it later?"

He shrugs apologetically. "I'm falling behind schedule."

My frown deepens. He's not giving in and I have no real right to tell him to stop. "How long are you going to be?"

He scratches his beard thoughtfully, making the muscles in his arms jump and I wonder what his beard would feel like scratching at my thighs.

"Just two more pieces to cut, and then I'm done."

It takes all my resolve to look him in the eye rather than devouring his body with my gaze, which is what I'm dying to do. It's hot outside, and I'm not sure if it's the sun or his body making me sweat.

"You're disturbing my book club."

He looks past me and smiles. "Doesn't seem like they mind too much."

I turn around to see my elderly patrons peering at us from the window with their faces pressed up against the glass. Janice waggles her fingers, and Kane waves back at her.

"Are you flirting with my customers?"

He chuckles. "They're flirting with me!"

"Just try to be quick," I say huffily.

"I'll take all the time I need." His eyes travel down my body as he says it, then flick back up to my face.

His gaze sets me on fire. My entire body tingles, and a blush creeps up my neck. I turn away quickly before he can see.

"Thank you," I say over my shoulder, striding back to the cafe.

As I walk in, the sawing starts up again. But there are no complaints from the ladies who keep their position watching Kane at his work.

I can't say I blame them, but I won't give him the satisfaction of joining them. I storm into the kitchen and whip up another batch of cookies, beating the mixture so hard it flies out of the bowl and onto the floor.

5

LAYLA

The next morning I'm late getting to the cafe. I rush around the corner and stop in my tracks. There's a line of women snaking down the road, white hair bobbing up and down as they chatter excitedly. There must be a sale on at the antique shop or something to attract this crowd.

"Excuse me," I say, squeezing past. As I get closer to the cafe, I see the line stops right outside the door to Books & Cookies. They're lining up for my cafe.

"Excuse me, I need to open up," I say to the first lady in the line.

"That's okay, dear. I hear the best view is outside anyway." She turns to her friend, and they both cackle with laughter.

"Best view of what?" I ask, but they just smile and raise their eyebrows at me.

I let the ladies in, and they file through the door as I switch on the lights and get the coffee machine going.

I'm glad I baked that extra batch of cookies yesterday, because there's no time for any baking this morning.

It's a chattier crowd than usual. They've come here to talk, not read. I spy Janice in the crowd, and even she doesn't seem to mind the talking.

"What's going on?" I ask her.

"They heard about your topless neighbor."

My mouth drops open. "They're here for Kane?"

She raises her eyebrows. "Oh yes."

I shake my head and get back to serving customers. Just before 10 a.m., a ripple of excitement runs through the room.

I look out the window, and Kane is striding over to the cafe. My stomach drops the way it always does when I see him, but this time I'm distracted by the commotion he's causing.

Ladies are pulling reading glasses out of handbags, smoothing down hair, and applying lipstick. You'd think they were at a high school dance and not a reading group for the over sixties.

He opens the door, and the chatter dies down immediately. Only Possum makes a mewling noise as he jumps off his perch on a coffee table to greet him.

Kane pats Possum and salutes Janice. He stops mid-salute as he notices the crowd of ladies watching him. They're not even pretending to be reading.

He looks around awkwardly, and it's the first time I've seen him disarmed. It's satisfying, and I can't help smirking.

"What can I get you today?" I say, folding my arms.

"Oh, are we allowed to talk today?" he asks, his easy smile back.

"Apparently so."

He looks down at the nearly empty counter and points to the last cookie. "I guess it's that one."

"And the usual coffee?"

"Please."

As I make his coffee, he looks around the shop awkwardly. "Busy book club today?"

"Something like that."

He hands over his money and I try not to touch him, but his hand brushes mine, and fudge biscuits, there it is again. That bolt of electricity that shoots up my arm whenever we touch. A delightful shiver that promises so much, making me think of those hands on my body, but also disappoints because I know it's just a fantasy.

I hand him his cookie, betraying nothing of the turmoil that's going on inside my body.

"Thanks," he says. But instead of going, he stands there looking at me for a moment. "Hey, do you want to come to my opening on Friday?"

My stomach lurches to the left, and I have to grip the countertop. I hear one of the ladies gasp.

"Umm." My mind is racing. I should say yes, but it's terrifying. "I'm working Friday."

One of the ladies makes a tutting noise.

"It's in the evening," says Kane, ignoring our audience. "Come along after you close up."

I glance over at Janice and she's nodding her head so hard I'm worried she'll give herself an injury.

He's only inviting me because it's the polite thing to do, invite your neighbor to your shop opening but these ladies think he's really asking me out. "Sure."

There's a collective sigh from the ladies, and I scan the shop to see big smiles and nods of encouragement. One old dear winks at me and gives me a thumbs up.

"Great," says Kane. "It starts at six."

He's about to turn around when a thought occurs to me. "What kind of shop is it?" He looks confused. "I don't know what it is you actually do."

"Woodwork. I make wooden furniture and ornaments. I build them and carve them."

"That explains the hands." I cover my mouth quickly; I wasn't meant to say that out loud.

He chuckles. "My hands are rough." His eyes sparkle with mischief and that look makes my core tug with a yearning I've never felt before. He leans forward and whispers so only I can hear, "But they're good for delicate work."

With a nod to the ladies, he strides out of the cafe.

I'm left with my mouth hanging open and my lady

cookie melting like chocolate in the sun. And from the looks that follow him out the door, I'd say I'm not the only one.

6

KANE

It's an hour until my grand opening when I place the final piece in the display cabinet. I was up till midnight doing the last coat of paint, and I've spent all day bringing in the merchandise with help from my brother.

I need to make this a success to pay off my bills and get business flowing again, or I'll have to close up for good.

The guest list includes anyone who's ever bought my work, along with local business owners and press. But the only concern running through my mind is whether Layla will show.

It's been a welcome distraction having the shop to do up, but every night when I fall exhausted into my bed, it's her I think about.

There's just time to duck home for a quick shower before the opening. With the water running over me, I think of Layla. I'm in crippling debt and about to go bankrupt but I've been spending my last dollars on a cookie and a coffee everyday just to spend a few minutes with her.

Her smile lights me up, her witty banter makes me chuckle and her curves, oh lordy, her curves make me want to push her up against the cafe wall and explore every delectable part of her. I long to run my hands over her soft skin, to press my lips against those perfect breasts and run my hand between her thighs. I think about her now, imagining her pretty eyes wide with pleasure as I tug at her nipples. I imagine her writhing against me and moaning as I sink into her.

I give myself a few hard tugs and find my release. But it's not satisfying; my body won't be satisfied until I have the real thing. I won't be satisfied until I make Layla mine.

I dress in dark suit pants and a crisp white shirt. I roll the sleeves up so my tattoos are visible at the wrists. A thin black tie hangs neatly under my rough beard.

I like the contrast; neat and messy, natural form and carved beauty. It makes me think of Layla again. Damn, I've got to get this woman out of my head, and there's only one way to do it. I have to make her mine tonight.

An hour later I'm greeting guests at the shop. Usually I love meeting my customers. It adds the personal touch to my work when I know who I'm making it for.

But tonight I can't concentrate on conversations. My gaze keeps shifting to the door, waiting for her to arrive.

"I want to talk to you about a piece for my wife."

I nod at the man in front of me. He's a local businessman who owns a ton of property and must be worth millions. "She wants something for the garden. Something unique she can show off at garden parties."

"I'm sure I can come up with something."

"She rather likes…"

I don't hear the rest of his sentence because suddenly Layla's at the door, peering in tentatively.

"Excuse me," I say, leaving the man staring after me.

I grab a glass of champagne from a tray and head to the door.

"Layla." I lean in to give her a kiss on the cheek, and she smells like fresh cookie dough and coffee. "You smell good enough to eat."

My lips brush her ear, and I'm sure I detect a shiver, which drives me wild. I'd love to know if I'm affecting this girl the way she's affecting me.

I pull away from the embrace and hand her the champagne. "What do you think?" I indicate the shop.

She looks around, her eyes wide. "It's looks amazing. I can't believe you've done all this in two weeks."

The entire wall in the middle of the shop has been knocked down with just a beam remaining. The shop is lined with display cases showing my smaller pieces, bookends, bowls, and cutting boards, the kind of purchases tourists stopping through might make.

I've installed a workbench running around two sides of the back of the shop. Tools hang from hooks, and half-finished pieces sit on the bench.

Wooden floorboards, newly polished, run throughout. There's a large coffee table with chairs that separates the work area from the shop, a place where customers can sit for a while and we can discuss what they want.

Her face falls when she sees the work bench. "You're going to be working here in the shop?"

I laugh, because I know exactly what she's thinking. "Don't worry. I've had it sound proofed."

"Sound proofed?" She looks confused.

"After your concerns on the first day we met, I adjusted the plans. It took a little longer, but I installed sound proofing in the walls. You won't hear a thing."

I don't tell her I had to extend my loan to cover the extra cost. It'll be worth it if it keeps her happy, and the smile she gives me lets me know I did the right thing.

"You did that for me?"

"Of course. I can't be responsible for scaring away your customers."

"Actually, I think you're responsible for attracting them to the cafe."

She tells me about the lines she's had all week, which makes me laugh. But I'm sure those old dears aren't just there to see me.

She takes a sip of champagne, and it fizzes onto her lips. Before I can stop myself, I dart out my tongue and lick the bubbles off her mouth, pressing my lips against hers.

She freezes, and I wonder if I've made a mistake. Then she kisses me back, and it's sweet and champagne sticky.

There's a click, and we jump apart. One of the reporters has her phone out snapping pictures of us.

"This is a great story, Kane, a nice love interest angle."

I smile at the reporter, hiding my irritation behind a good-natured smile. "It's my opening. I'm celebrating," I say, holding up the champagne.

Layla looks worried, and I take her hand in mine and give it a squeeze.

"Who's your girlfriend?" asks the reporter.

I hesitate. I want more than anything for Layla to be my girlfriend, but not like this. Not as part of a press circus to make a good story.

At that moment, there's a shriek from across the room.

"Ohh, Kane. I loooove it!"

Belinda Brown is strolling across the room, faux-fur shawl flapping across her otherwise bare shoulders, six-inch heels clacking on my newly polished wooden floors.

She pulls me into a warm embrace, and I feel Layla's hand leave mine.

He goes serious all of a sudden, and his eyes look black in the dim light. "I've known since the first day you strode into my shop that you were the woman for me, Layla. Confident, sassy, beautiful."

"Go on," I say.

He laughs. "Modest too." He casts his gaze down my body. "Not to mention this delicious body I'm dying to get my hands on."

He takes a step closer, and I can smell wood oil and champagne and sawdust.

"Is that chocolate and caramel?" He sniffs the cookie dough on my hands.

I nod. "Chocolate and salted caramel."

"May I?" Without waiting for an answer, he leans in and licks the sticky dough off my little finger.

His rough tongue and warm breath set my skin on fire. I watch, fascinated, as he moves onto my ring finger. His mouth encloses around it and he sucks the dough off, sending shock waves tingling down the nerves under my skin and throughout my entire body.

He's looking at me with a cheeky sparkle in his eye as he moves to my middle finger.

"Mmm, tastes good."

I close my eyes and tilt my head back as his mouth works its way down every finger of my hand. By the time he's gotten to my thumb, my legs are like jelly biscuits, and my panties are as wet as sticky sauce.

Then he starts on my other hand, and all I can do is whimper.

This time as he sucks my fingers, his hand slides up my skirt. I feel every rough callous against my soft thigh, and it's as hot as I imagined it would be. He gets to my panties and I'm embarrassed by how wet they are, but when he touches the dampness, he lets out a deep rumbling groan.

"Oh girl, you're wet for me."

I gurgle in response, because my bits are on fire and I seem to have lost the power of speech. Then his hand pulls my panties aside, and those rough fingertips are brushing at my hair and teasing my folds.

"Wait," I gasp, and he stops immediately.

"Everything okay? Am I moving too fast?" He slides his hand out from under my skirt.

"Don't do that," I say, snapping my knees together and trapping his hand. "Put it back."

He looks at me quizzically and slides his hand slowly back up my thigh. "Then what is it, baby girl? Tell me what you want?"

He talks slow and deep and it's almost the undoing of me, but I have to tell him. "I'm a virgin," I blurt out.

His hand stops, his fingers brushing the edge of my panties. "Oh, baby girl."

"Is that bad?"

"No, no." A grin spreads over his face. "That's perfect. Just perfect."

His hand slides out from my leg.

"It doesn't mean you have to stop," I say, panic rising in my voice. He's unleashed feelings in me I never knew he had and all I want is for him to keep going.

"I want to make it perfect for your first time. Let's go back to my place."

"No," I say. I take his hand in mine and run it up my leg to the hot wet place. "Don't stop, please."

He groans. "Oh, baby girl, if that's what you want."

"Yes. Yes, that's what I want."

8

KANE

My mouth crashes into Layla's. Our tongues collide, and I suck hungrily at her soft lips. She tastes of sugar and rich chocolate, and I harden instantly. I press against her, pushing her backwards until her ass collides with the counter.

I slide my hands under her ass and lift her up. She lets out a squeal, and I put her down on the countertop.

"You okay, baby girl?"

"Better than okay," she say breathlessly.

Her chest is heaving, and suddenly I need to get my hands on those breasts. I rip open her blouse, sending buttons pinging around the shop. There's an irritated yowl as one of them hits Possum.

Layla giggles, and it turns into a moan as I rub my hand over her chest, sliding it into her bra to cup her soft breast.

I reach my other hand around to undo the bra, and

it drops onto the counter. Her breasts are like milky orbs in the darkness of the shop. I close my eyes and rub my beard over them, breathing in their sugary smell of cookie dough and sweet sweat.

My lips play over the soft skin, and I take a nipple in my mouth, biting it gently. She takes a sharp intake of breath.

"That too rough for you, baby girl?"

"If that's rough, then I think I like it rough."

"Whatever you want."

I give her other nipple a squeeze as I run my teeth over her skin. Her moans tell me all I need to know.

Working slowly, I make my way down Layla's soft body, licking and sucking every inch of her, always keeping one hand tweaking that nipple.

By the time I get to her belly button, she's writhing on the counter.

"Keep going," she whispers. "Lower."

I chuckle. "Oh, baby girl." She's bold, and it makes me want her even more. I slide her skirt up, and her panties are dripping wet. "I'll take care of you."

My fingers pull her panties aside, and I kneel in front of her. In the darkness I can make out her glistening pink folds. My dick aches to be inside her, and I undo my fly, giving it some space.

I slide my tongue up her thigh until I reach her wet button. Her tangy candy smell sends pre-cum shooting out of me. And her taste—it's the sweetest cookie a man could ever want.

I lick her hungrily, lapping up every last drop of her sweet sauce. She leans forward and takes my head in her hands, pulling me towards her. I can still reach her breasts and I keep one hand on her nipple, squeezing and tugging as I lick her until she's moaning my name.

Suddenly there's a gush of wetness, and she cries out as the orgasm shakes her body.

I lick her slowly until I sense her release end. When I glance up, Layla's looking at me with dreamy eyes.

"I never knew it would feel that good."

"I'm not done with you yet." I get to my feet and slide my pants off. Her eyes go wide when she sees my dick standing tall and proud. "You ready for me, baby girl?"

"Oh yeah." She wraps her legs around my waist and pulls me toward her. I'm lined up with her slit, and I rub my tip across her entrance, enjoying the jolts of sensation that shoot through me.

"Shouldn't we use a condom?" she says.

"If you want, baby girl. But I know you're the woman for me. I want to plant my seed in you. I want to make you mine forever."

Her eyes widen and she bites her lower lip. "I want that too."

She's looking at me with big wide eyes, but I can tell there's something else. "What is it?" I ask.

"What if you're too big?" she whispers.

"I'll take it slow," I tell her, easing my tip into her entrance. "Like this."

Her eyelids flutter as I slide myself into her folds. She tilts her head back, which lifts her breasts right into my face, and it takes all my resolve to stop. My dick's throbbing, and I want to thrust it in and claim what's mine. But I make myself wait.

My mouth licks her nipple making her shudder as I slide in a bit more.

I stop as I bump up against her hymen. "Almost there, baby girl." I slide back out and in again, pausing at the hymen, her pussy sucking me in like a moist, warm vice.

Layla moans, and this time I can't hold back. I thrust hard, bursting through her virgin barrier. She cries out, tensing her grip around me.

"That's it, baby girl." I groan as we rock together, locked together with the sweetest sensations shooting through me.

When I sense her relax, I move slowly, sinking deeper and deeper into my woman. Each time she glides down my shaft it's like a bolt of pleasure running through my body.

I know I'm not going to last long fucking this sweet goddess. She's too damn sexy with her breasts bouncing in my face and those high-pitched moans she's making.

I pull her down my shaft, making sure to hit her sweet spot with every thrust. I can't hold back much longer. Each time I slam into her, her body jolts and she cries out.

"That's it, baby girl, come for me."

Layla's cries turn to squeals and I explode inside her, my cum shooting deep into her womb, the sweet release draining out of me and filling her up.

Our sweaty bodies remain entwined until long after we both finish coming. She feels so good pressed against me that I don't want to pull apart.

"Will it always feel this good?" she asks.

I kiss the top of her head. "It will always feel this good to be with you."

Layla slides off the counter, and I help her get dressed. She's suddenly shy sliding her bra back on, and I take her hand.

"I meant what I said. You're my woman now and forever." I kiss her gently. "Now let's go back to my place, and I'll show you how it's done in a bed."

I pull her close to me, and I know without a doubt that I'm holding my future wife in my arms. And just maybe our child is already growing inside her.

EPILOGUE

LAYLA

Six years later...

I pull the tray out of the oven and breathe in the smell of baked chocolate.

"Can I have one, Momma?"

A little hand reaches up for the hot tray, and I bat it away. "Not until they're cool, sweetheart."

Nikki folds her arms and pouts at me in the way only a three-year-old can. "But I want one now."

I bend down so I'm at her height. "You'll just have to wait."

"But Daddy gets to eat one."

I spin around to find Kane with a cookie in his hands, bouncing it between the tips of his fingers. "Ow, these are hot."

"These are for customers," I say, smiling. "Not for you lot."

He gives me a quick kiss. "I can never resist your cookie," he murmurs into my ear.

I bat him away playfully, letting out an involuntary giggle. Our daughter is watching us with folded arms, the pout even bigger than before.

Kane bends down and breaks his cookie in half. "Here you go, Nikki," he says solemnly. "You can have half of Daddy's."

She smiles widely and gives him a hug before snatching the cookie and skipping off to the back of the cafe. It seems the way to our daughter's heart is through her stomach, just like her father.

Kane slides his arm around me and rubs my pregnant belly. "You should be resting."

"I'm fine. In fact, I'm feeling quite energetic," I add with a whisper. "If you know what I mean."

He raises his eyebrows at me. "I believe I do know what you mean."

"Keep it down, you two." We jump apart at the reprimand from Janice, who's sitting in her favorite armchair. But she's smiling at us, her eyes twinkling. Her book is face down on the table, and instead of reading she's holding a miniature teacup as Grace solemnly pours imaginary tea into it.

The cafe is full of our regular customers. After Kane and I got together, the Romance Reading group kept growing. It seems they were interested in the real-life romance unfolding in front of them.

Janice came to our wedding a few months later, and

once Nikki was born, the added attraction of having a baby in the cafe endeared our regulars to us even more. Grace has an extended family of grandmas, and we're never short of a babysitter.

We still have the cafe and shop side by side. We opened up the entrance so one doorway leads to both shops, and we run them together. Customers stop by for coffee and cookies after they've perused Kane's woodwork.

We both have assistants now who help run the place, so Kane has more time to create and I have move time to bake.

Nikki runs between the two shops. She's fascinated by her daddy's workshop and will sit for hours watching him work. Seems she's more interested in woodwork than cookies, except for eating them, of course.

I slide the cookies onto the cooling rack and can't help taking one for myself too. I'm constantly hungry at this stage of pregnancy, and my tastes buds seem heightened. As the gooey warm chocolate hits the back of my throat I let out a moan.

"If you keep doing that, I'm definitely going to have to take you home," whispers Kane.

Janice looks up from her tea party. "If you two have any errands you need to run, I'm happy to watch Grace," she says innocently.

"Thanks," says Kane quickly. "We do have an errand."

"We need to get to the, ah, post office," I say.

Kane grabs my hand, practically drags me out the door.

"Don't rush back," Janice calls after us, a big grin on her face.

We laugh as we stumble out of the shop hand in hand. He squeezes my hand, and the rough calluses against my soft skin set a fire burning between my legs.

"You are gonna get it good when we get home."

"Who says anything about going home?"

He pulls me into his shop, and we go through to the storeroom out the back.

It's dark and dirty, and the perfect place for a quickie. He pushes me against the hard bench, sending tools and paintbrushes toppling. As he hikes my skirt up around my waist, I'm already dripping wet.

"Get ready, baby girl, 'cause I need my fix."

He thrusts into me, and I groan with pleasure. He's holding my ass in his hands as he pushes deeper inside, the rhythm building to a quick pace as he slams into me. The bench shakes with every thrust, and I bite my lip so as not to cry out.

It doesn't take long till I feel him explode inside me. I let myself go, my orgasm shaking my body and my pussy pulsing around him.

We hold each other for a long moment, panting and satisfied.

"We better get back to the shop," I say.

"Not yet. We don't want Janice to think we're that quick."

I laugh.

"And besides," he says, nibbling at my neck, "I'm not done with you yet." As his mouth moves down to my sensitive breasts, I lean back and bask in the wonderful sensation of my man pleasuring me. Feeling safe and beautiful and like the luckiest girl in the world.

GET YOUR FREE BOOK

Sign up to the Sadie King mailing list for a FREE book!

You'll be the first to hear about exclusive offers, bonus content and all the news from Sadie King.

Allie is a bonus book in the Curvy Girl Can series exclusive to my newsletter subscribers.

To claim your free book visit:
authorsadieking.com/bonus-scenes

ABOUT THE AUTHOR

Sadie King is a USA Today Best Selling Author of short instalove romance.

She lives in New Zealand with her ex-military husband and raucous young son.

When she's not writing she loves catching waves with her son, running along the beach, and drinking good wine, preferably with a book in hand.